15 Easy-to-Read

Folk & Fairy Tale
Mini-Books

By Liza Charlesworth • Illustrations by Patrick Girouard

SCHOLASTIC
PROFESSIONAL BOOKS

New York • Toronto • London • Auckland • Sydney • New Delhi • Mexico City • Hong Kong

Dedication

To Aesop, the Brothers Grimm, Hans Christian Andersen,
and the prolific anonymous—
who invented, embellished, and committed
these important tales to paper.

Illustrations by Patrick Girouard
Cover design by James Sarfati
Design by Grafica, Inc.

ISBN: 0-439-22730-5
Copyright © 2001 by Liza Charlesworth.

Contents

Teaching With Classic Stories

Introduction

 *nce upon a time . . .*

This well-worn opening line has enchanted children around the world for hundreds of years. And today's generation is no exception. Classic stories—fairy tales, folk tales, and fables—are still a joyful rite of passage for every young learner. These timeless tales invite kids to turn off the TV or step away from the computer for a few minutes to savor a rollicking  good yarn with a meaningful message. After all, who can resist the tenacious Little Red Hen, the foolhardy Big Bad Wolf, the endearing Ugly Duckling? Nothing compares to the place an imagination roams during the reading of a cherished story!

15 Easy-to-Read Folk & Fairy Tale Mini-Books was created to put those stories in the hands of every child you teach. Research shows that when kids are actively engaged in quality literature, they are motivated to read. And the more they read, the more confident they become. What better way to engage your students than with eye-widening, giggle-inducing classic tales? Each of these illustrated mini-storybooks contains simple, age-appropriate text and lots of predictable language to provide a powerful step up to young readers at every level—from emergent to fluent. And here's more good news: Their reproducible format means you'll be able to send them home for children to enjoy with the folks they love.

Here's hoping that these little books set your students on the path to reading . . . *happily ever after.*

Making the Mini-Storybooks

These mini-storybooks are a snap to assemble. Just follow these simple directions:

1. Make a double-sided photocopy of the mini-storybook pages. (Note that some books will require two sheets of paper; see list below.)

2. Cut the sheet (or sheets) in half along the solid line.

3. If books are made from one double-sided sheet of paper, place spread A on top of B. If books are made from two double-sided sheets of paper, place spread C on top of D; then place A and B on top of them in sequence.

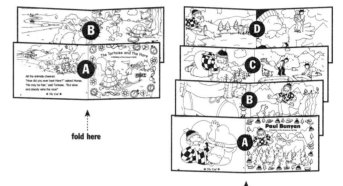

Short Mini-Books   **Long Mini-Books**

fold here

4. Fold the pages in half along the dashed line.

5. Make sure the pages are in the proper order. Then staple them together along the book's spine.

fold here

6. Invite kids to color in the pictures.

**Short Mini-Books
(Books that require
one sheet of paper)**

The Gingerbread Man
The Little Red Hen
The Lion and the Mouse
The Tortoise and the Hare
The Princess and the Pea
The Ugly Ducking
There Was a Crooked Man
Poems for Your Pocket

**Long Mini-Books
(Books that require
two sheets of paper)**

The Three Little Pigs
The Three Billy Goats Gruff
Goldilocks and the Three Bears
Paul Bunyan
The Emperor's New Clothes
The Fisherman and His Wife
The Bremen Town Musicians

Building Literacy Skills With Mini-Storybooks

Make mini-storybooks a part of your classroom routine, and you'll have the double-benefit of building reading skills as you expose kids to important cultural touch-stones. These easy-to-read stories are perfect for:

- Shared reading
- Buddy reading
- Independent reading
- Guided reading
- Take-home reading

In addition, here are some instant ideas to maximize learning mileage:

Once-Upon-a-Time Word Wall

Nurture reading, writing, spelling, and vocabulary skills by creating a special word wall just for folk and fairy tales! Designate a bulletin board, or, better yet, cut a giant ginger-bread man shape out of craft paper, hang it on the wall, and use it to display the special words and terms associated with classic stories—*once upon a time, happily ever after, by and by, emperor, cozy, magic, cottage, three,* and so on.

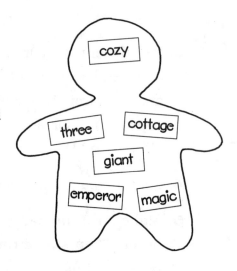

Folk and Fairy Tale Listening Center

To help your youngest learners gain reading independence, create a Folk and Fairy Tale Listening Center, where children can hear the stories on tape as they scan the text in the books. To make the tales extra compelling, add some simple sound effects or distinctive voices for the dialogue segments.

Shoe Box Personal Libraries

Invite students to decorate shoe boxes with favorite folk and fairy tale characters to house their collections. Having a personal book set enables children to return to the tales again and again for practice and pure enjoyment.

Send-Home Reading Badges

Encouraging children to share these classic stories with their families will give them a golden opportunity to show off their reading know-how. If students are confident readers and are familiar with the story, reproduce and pin the "Let Me Read _____ to You!" badge to their shirts; if students are less-confident readers and the story is still a bit challenging, use the "Let's Read _____ Together!" badge. Either way, you're sure to spur at-home reading enthusiasm and reinforce important literacy skills in the process.

6

Let Me
Read
_____
to You!

Let's
Read.
_____
Together!

Exploring Story Elements

A firm grasp of the elements of story enables young learners to become more effective readers and writers—and helps you assess their comprehension. Use the mini-storybooks and the reproducible Story Elements graphic organizer on page 9 to reinforce these essential concepts. Invite students to record the main characters and the setting of a particular tale, then to retell the plot by chunking it into a bite-sized beginning, middle, and end. Kids can respond in words, pictures, or a combination of the two. For added fun, encourage kids to rate the story by coloring in one to five magic wands.

Comparing and Contrasting Tales

An easy and fun way to practice the skill of comparing literature is to look for similarities and differences between two tales. To do this, draw a Venn diagram on the board or a sheet of chart paper, labeling each circle with the name of a different story. Then, working with your class, record in the appropriate spot the ways the stories are alike and unlike. When you are done, reflect on your data—you may be surprised at what you discover!

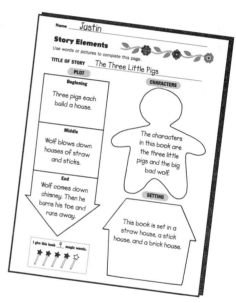

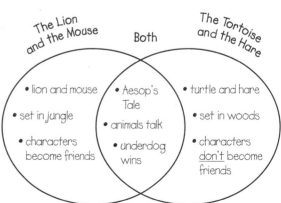

Highlighting Moral Lessons

The Brothers Grimm published stories in the early 1800s, whereas the fables of Aesop date back more than 2,500 years. One reason these tales have flourished is that many present timeless moral lessons. What can we learn from "The Fisherman and His Wife" or "The Lion and the Mouse"? How are these stories relevant to kids' own lives and to your classroom? Invite children to discuss and/or write about their thoughts in journals. If you like, make a chart that lists the main message of each tale. Are there any messages that children disagree with? What do these stories tell us about the gender roles of boys and girls in the era in which these tales were created? Have times changed?

Inviting Children to Write Original Tales

Once children have read their way through the mini-storybook collection, they'll have a solid understanding of the "rules" of classic stories. What better way for kids to show what they know than to craft and illustrate original tales? Before students sit down to write, go over the common elements of the folk and fairy tales you've read—for example, most begin with "Once upon a time," many feature talking animals, a lot include the number three, all of them teach a lesson. Then invite children to use the writing process—plan, write, revise, edit, publish—to arrive at a thoughtful, polished final product. When children have completed their writing, host an author tea in which kids share their stories and munch on—what else!—favorite-character cookies.

Name _____

Story Elements

Use words or pictures to complete this page.

TITLE OF STORY _____

PLOT

Beginning

Middle

End

CHARACTERS

SETTING

I give this book _____ magic wands.

9

Traditional

Mini-Books

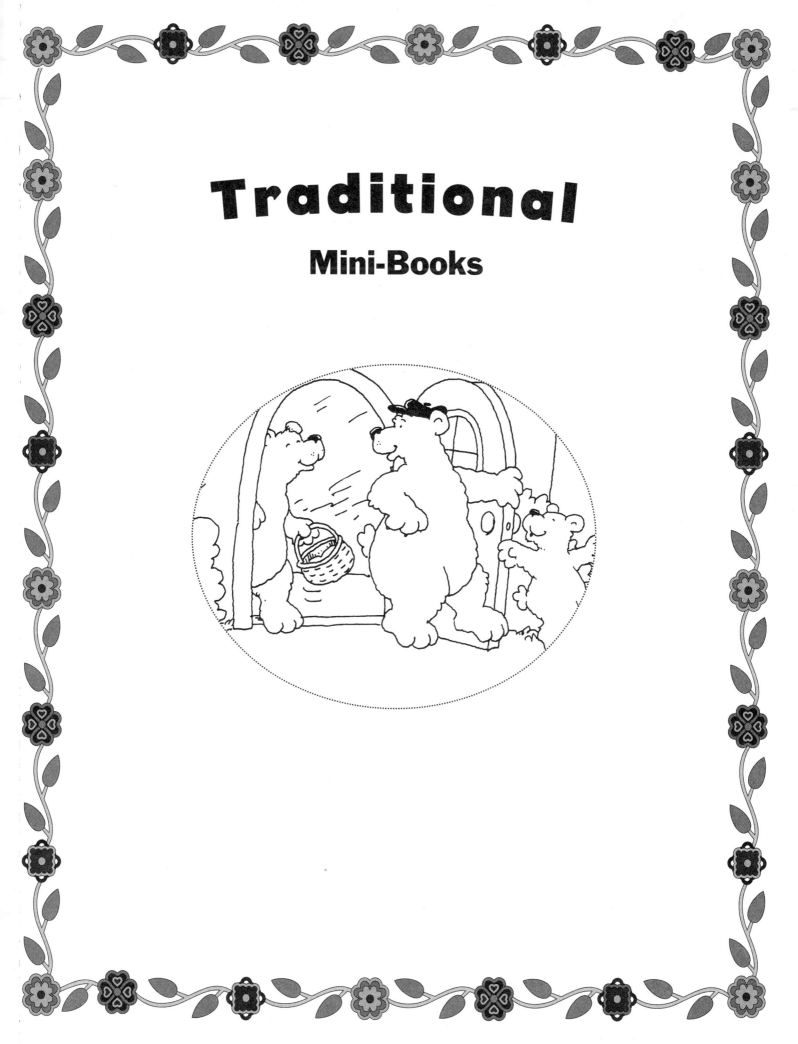

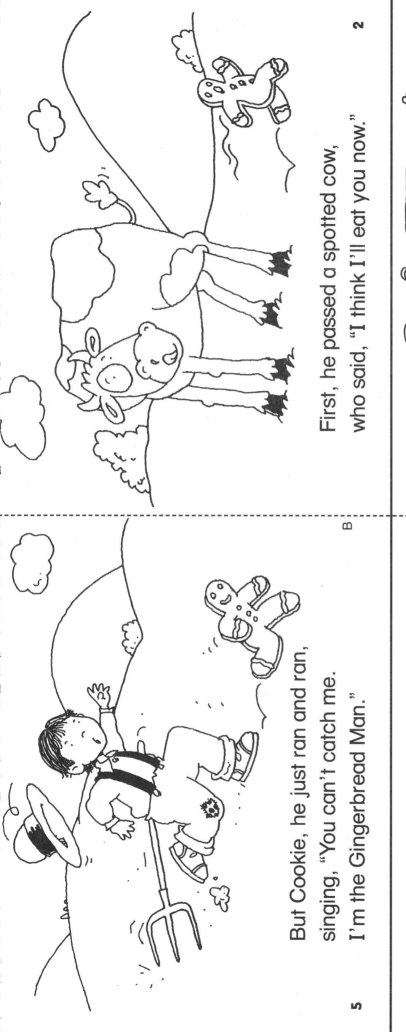

2

First, he passed a spotted cow, who said, "I think I'll eat you now."

B

The Gingerbread Man

A Retelling of the Traditional Tale

A

But Cookie, he just ran and ran, singing, "You can't catch me. I'm the Gingerbread Man."

5

When the Cookie shouted, "Yes, oh yes!" The wise fox ate him. Did you guess?

❀ *The End* ❀

7

But Cookie, he just ran and ran,
singing, "You can't catch me.
I'm the Gingerbread Man."

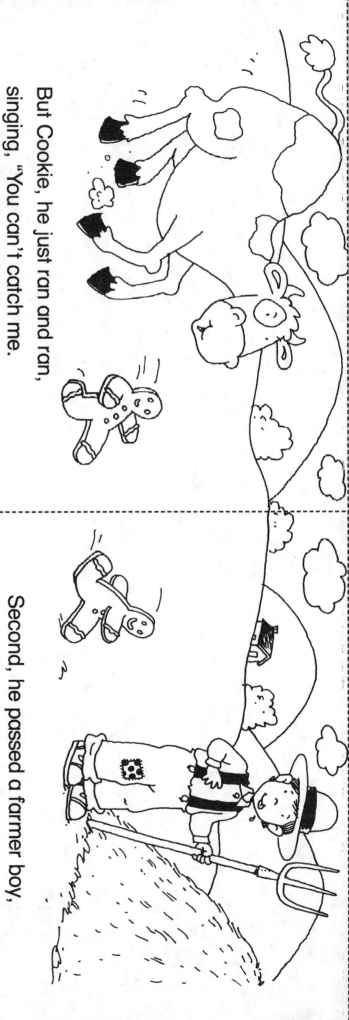

Second, he passed a farmer boy,
who said, "I'll eat you, what a joy!"

A cookie jumped right off the pan.
The door was open so out he ran.

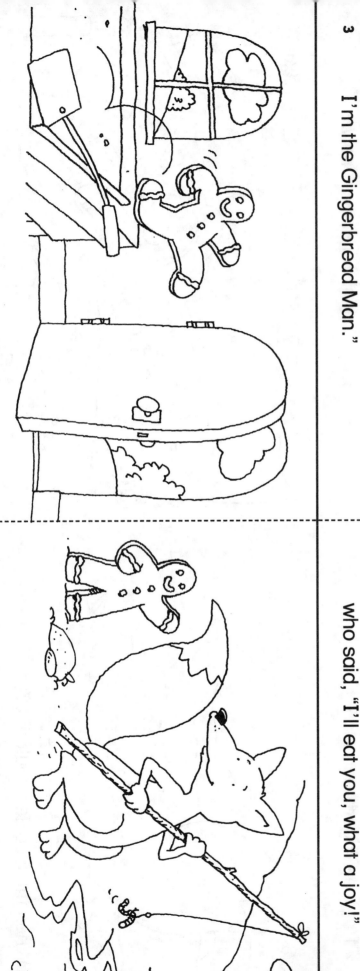

Third, he reached a river wide,
where a fox said, "Would you like a ride?"

The Three Little Pigs

A Retelling of the Traditional Tale

One day, each pig decided to build a house to keep safe from the big bad wolf. You see, the wolf loved to eat little pigs!

When the wolf put his big toe in the pot, boy did he yell.

After that, the three little pigs lived safe and snug in the cozy house of bricks. And the big bad wolf never bothered them again.

❀ The End ❀

3

The first little pig built a cozy
house of straw.

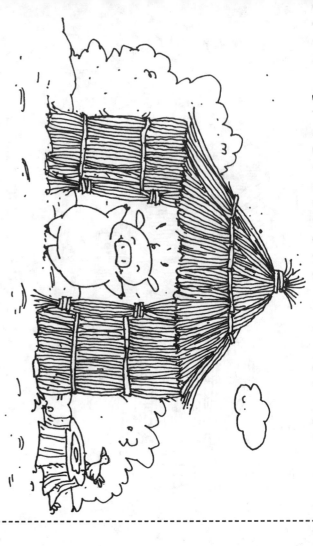

"Do drop in!" said the pigs sweetly.
You see, they had put a pot of
super-hot water at the bottom.

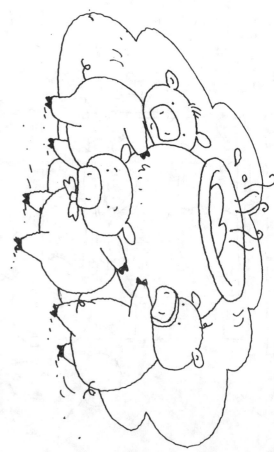

12

1

Once upon a time, there were
three little pigs.

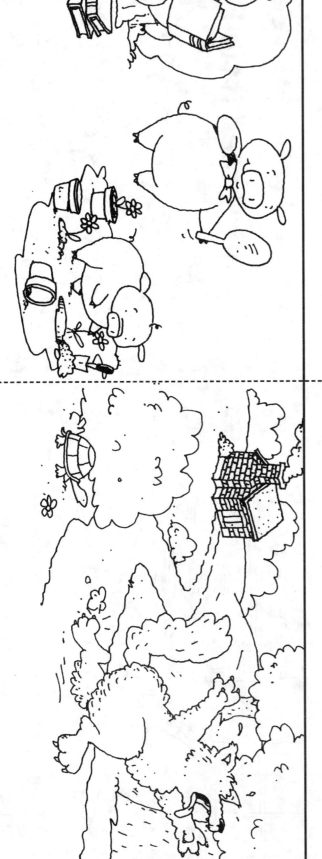

Then, quick as a wink, he jumped out
the chimney and ran far, far away.

14

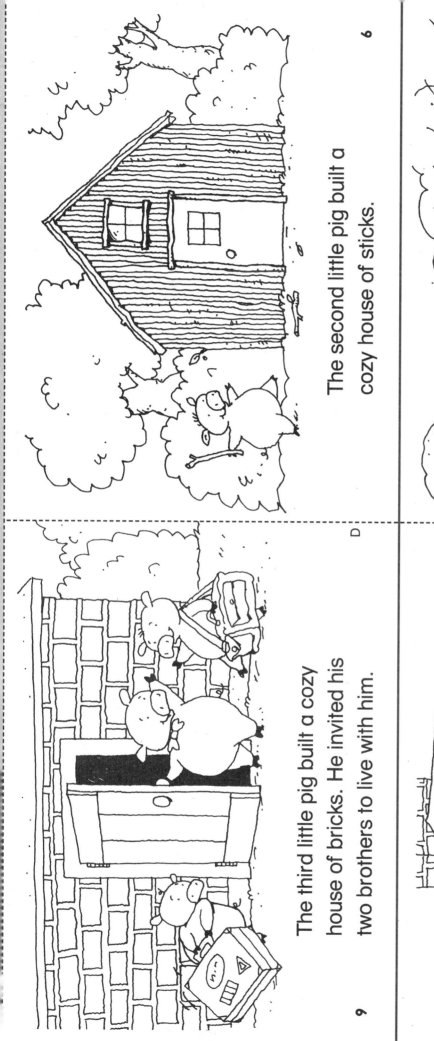

The second little pig built a cozy house of sticks.

6

D

But the big bad wolf huffed and puffed and blew it down!

4

C

The third little pig built a cozy house of bricks. He invited his two brothers to live with him.

9

"I'm coming down the chimney to eat you for dinner!" he said.

11

But the big bad wolf huffed
and puffed and blew it down!

Quick as a wink, the second little pig
ran away before he became lunch.

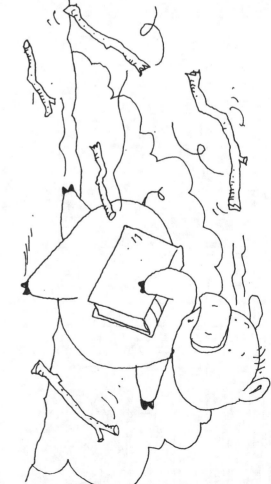

Quick as a wink, the first little pig ran
away before he became breakfast.

The big bad wolf huffed and puffed
and huffed and puffed. But he just
couldn't blow the brick house down.

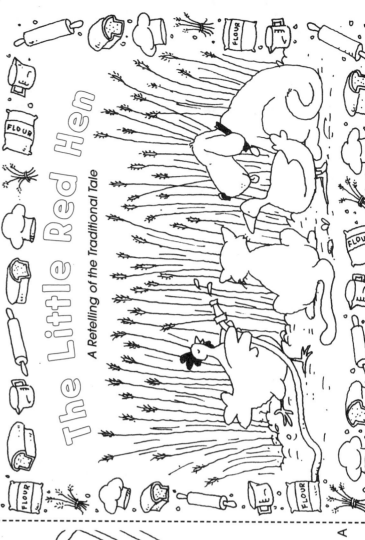

The Little Red Hen

A Retelling of the Traditional Tale

A

"Not us," said lazy Dog and Cat and Duck.

"I will just have to do it myself," she said.

2

B

Before long, all the wheat was cut.

"Who will help me make this into bread?"

asked Little Red Hen.

5

Before long, all the bread was baked.

"Who will help me eat this?" asked Little Red Hen.

"Us!" said hungry Dog and Cat and Duck.

"Nope, I will just have to do it myself," she said.

❋ *The End* ❋

7

Before long, all the wheat was tall.
"Who will help me cut this?" asked
Little Red Hen.

3

"Not us," said lazy Dog and Cat and Duck.
"I will just have to do it myself," she said.

4

Once upon a time, the Little Red Hen
decided to plant some wheat.
"Who will help me plant this?" she asked.

1

"Not us," said lazy Dog and Cat and Duck.
"I will just have to do it myself," she said.

6

One day, they decided to cross the bridge to eat the sweet green grass on the other side.

2

The Three Billy Goats Gruff

A Retelling of the Traditional Tale

A

"Stop there! I am going to eat you up!" yelled Troll.

13 "Okay," said Big Billy, for he had a sneaky plan.

B

After that, the three brothers crossed the bridge whenever they liked. And, my, was that sweet green grass delicious!

❀ *The End* ❀

15

There was only one problem. A mean troll lived under it.

Once upon a time, there lived three billy goat brothers: Little Billy, Middle Billy, and Big Billy.

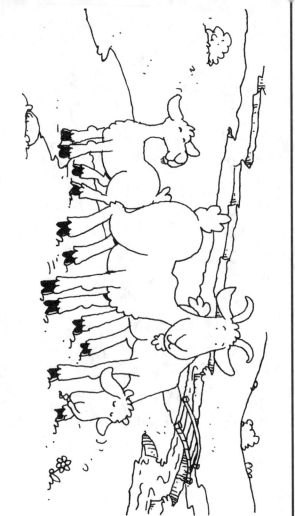

CLOMP, CLOMP, CLOMP! Big Billy started across the bridge. Then he heard a craggy voice.

When Troll climbed onto the bridge, Big Billy butted him so hard that he fell in the water with a giant SPLASH!

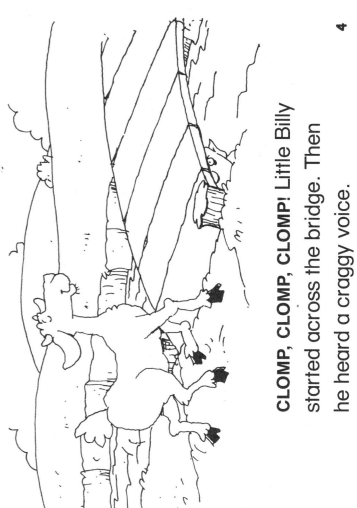

"Wait for my brother. He is bigger and much more delicious than I!" cried Little Billy.

6

D

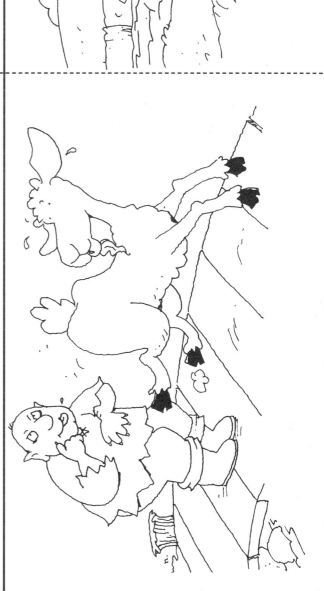

CLOMP, CLOMP, CLOMP! Little Billy started across the bridge. Then he heard a craggy voice.

4

C

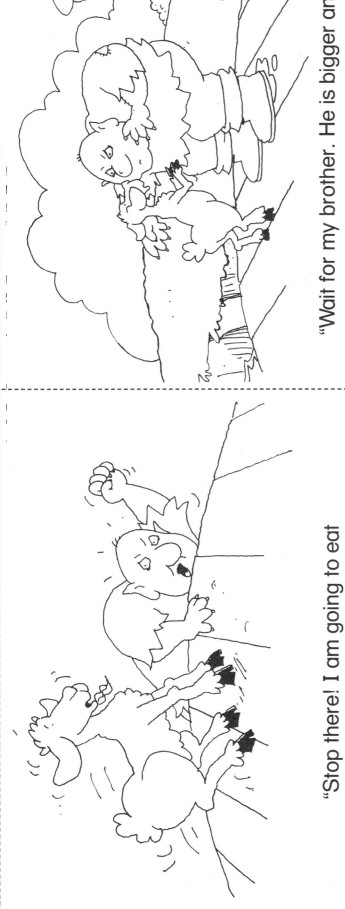

"Stop there! I am going to eat you up!" yelled Troll.

9

"What a fine idea," said Troll, licking his lips.
And with that, Middle Billy crossed the bridge.

11

"What a fine idea," said Troll, licking his lips.

And with that, Little Billy crossed the bridge.

7

CLOMP, CLOMP, CLOMP! Middle Billy started across the bridge. Then he heard a craggy voice.

8

"Stop there! I am going to eat you up!" yelled Troll.

5

"Wait for my brother. He is bigger and much more delicious than I!" cried Middle Billy.

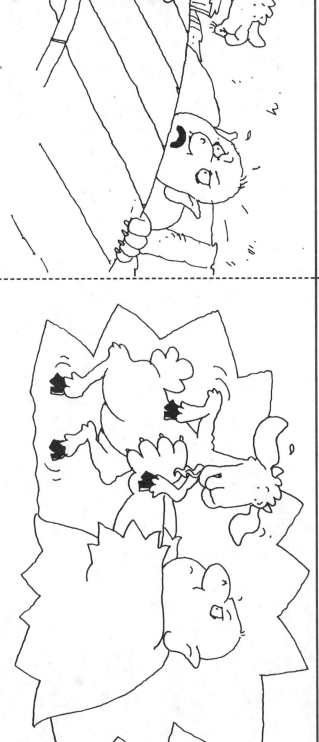

10

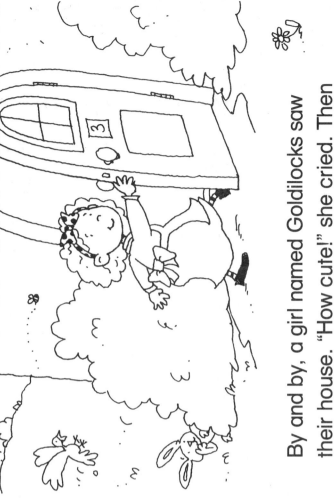

By and by, a girl named Goldilocks saw their house. "How cute!" she cried. Then she opened the door and went inside.

2

B

Goldilocks and the Three Bears

A Retelling of the Traditional Tale

A

The bears went into the bedroom to lie down. "Someone has been sleeping in our beds!" growled Papa Bear and Mama Bear.

13

B

Just then, Goldilocks opened her eyes. Yikes! She was so scared that she jumped up and ran out the door. And the three bears never saw that troublesome girl again.

❋ *The End* ❋

15

A

3

In the kitchen, Goldilocks found three fine bowls of porridge. She tried the big bowl. It was too hot. She tried the middle bowl. It was too cold.

12

"And someone broke mine to bits!" growled Baby Bear.

1

One bright day, the three bears decided to go for a walk. They closed the door of their tidy house and set out into the sunshine.

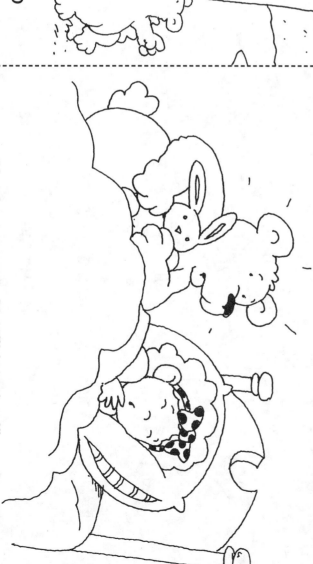

"And someone is still in mine!" growled Baby Bear.

14

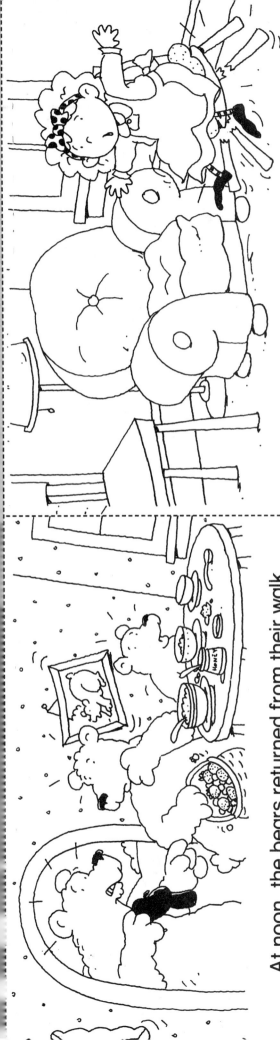

Finally, she tried the little chair. It was just right, so she sat right down. But the chair broke into bits. Crrrack!

6

D

Finally, she tried the little bowl. It was just right, so she ate it up. Slurrrp!

4

C

At noon, the bears returned from their walk and went into the kitchen to have lunch. "Someone has been eating our porridge!" growled Papa Bear and Mama Bear.

9

The bears went into the living room to sit down. "Someone has been sitting in our chairs!" growled Papa Bear and Mama Bear.

11

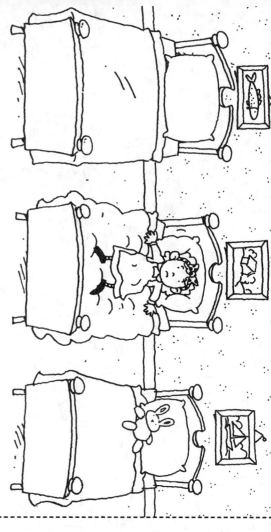

7

In the bedroom, Goldilocks found three fine beds. She tried the big one. It was too hard. She tried the middle bed. It was too soft.

In the living room, Goldilocks found three fine chairs. She tried the big chair. It was too hard. She tried the middle chair. It was too soft.

5

Finally, she tried the little bed. Why, it was just right, so she lay down and went to sleep. Zzzzzz!

8

"And someone ate mine all up!" growled Baby Bear.

10

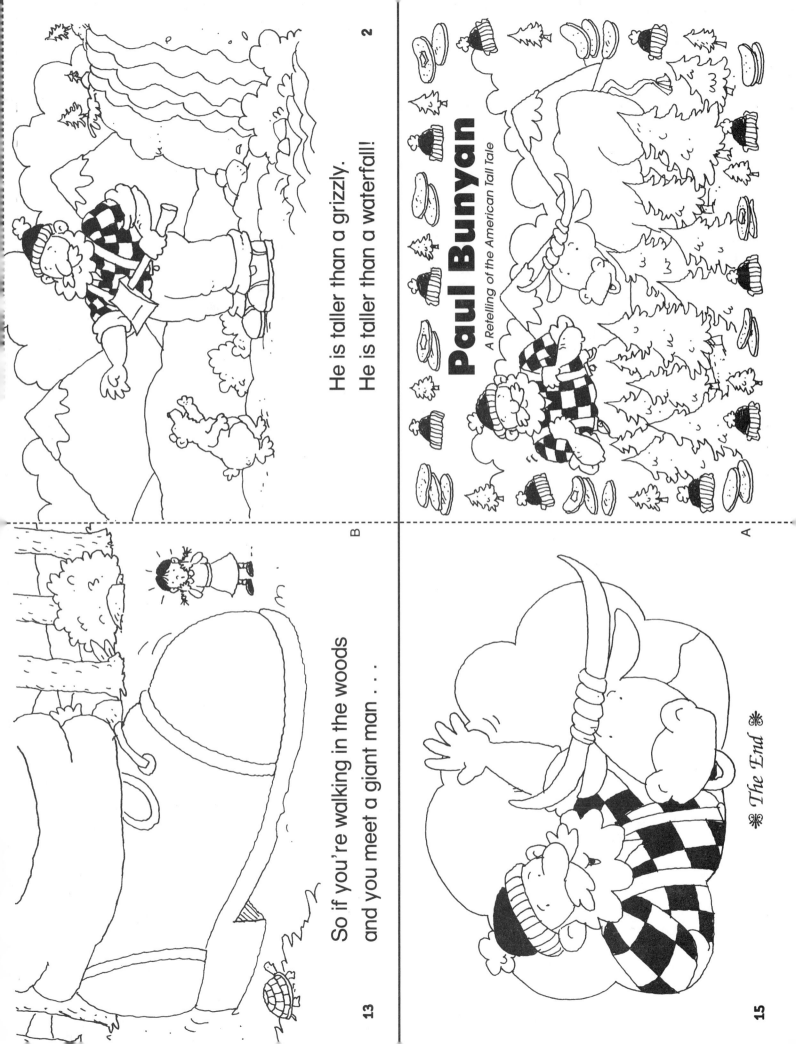

He is taller than a grizzly.
He is taller than a waterfall!

2

B

Paul Bunyan
A Retelling of the American Tall Tale

A

So if you're walking in the woods
and you meet a giant man . . . .

13

❄ *The End* ❄

15

3

He is taller than a redwood.
In fact, his head, it scrapes the sky!

12

He can eat 500 pancakes
and 1,000 bowls of stew!

1

Paul Bunyan is quite a hero,
and is he ever tall!

14

Shout "hello" to big Paul Bunyan—
he'll bend down to shake your hand!

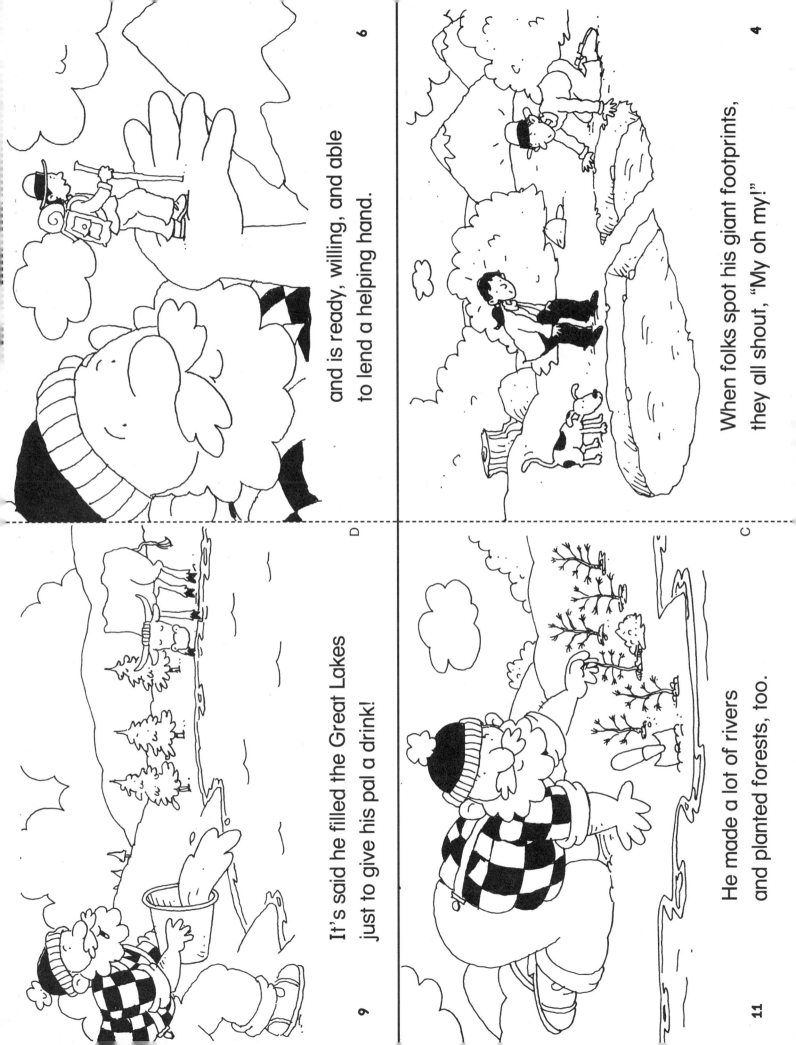

and is ready, willing, and able
to lend a helping hand.

6

D

When folks spot his giant footprints,
they all shout, "My oh my!"

4

C

It's said he filled the Great Lakes
just to give his pal a drink!

9

He made a lot of rivers
and planted forests, too.

11

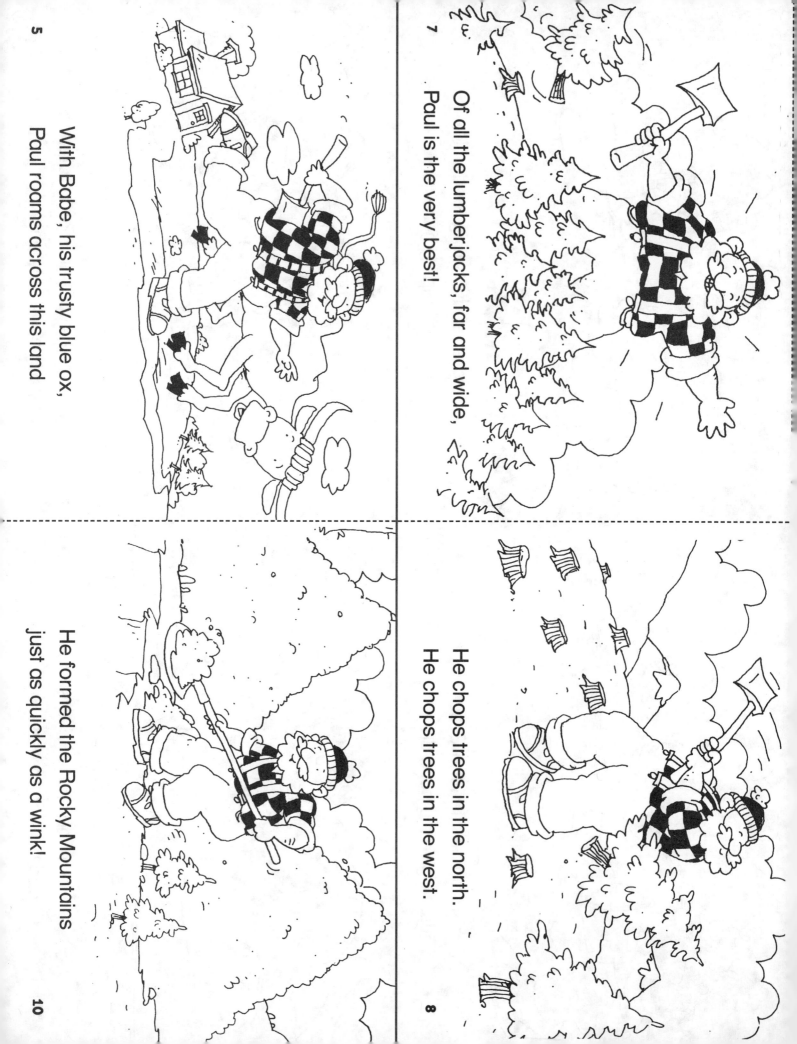

Of all the lumberjacks, far and wide,
Paul is the very best!

With Babe, his trusty blue ox,
Paul roams across this land

He chops trees in the north.
He chops trees in the west.

He formed the Rocky Mountains
just as quickly as a wink!

Aesop's Fables
Mini-Books

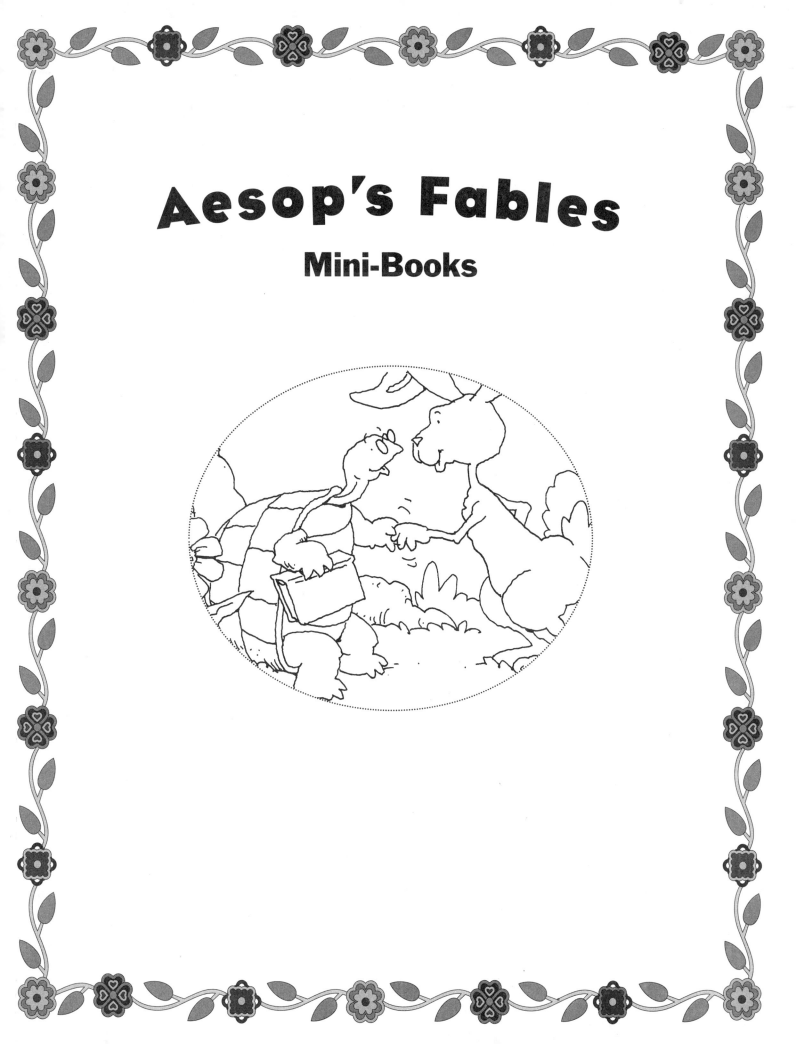

"Please let me go," squeaked the
mouse. "Someday I can help you."

2

B

The Lion and the Mouse

A Retelling of the Aesop's Fable

A

A few days later, the grateful mouse saw a
surprising sight. The lion was caught in a
hunter's net! "Help me!" roared the lion.

5

From that day on, the lion never doubted that a
teeny weeny mouse could be a great big help.

※ *The End* ※

7

3

The lion laughed very hard. How could a teeny weeny mouse ever help a great big lion?

1

Once upon a time, a great big lion caught a teeny weeny mouse.

4

"You are so funny that I WILL let you go," said the lion. Then he lifted his paw, and the mouse scurried away.

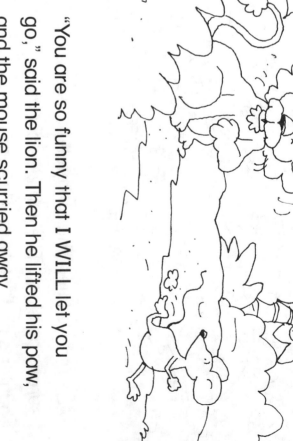

6

The mouse chewed and chewed and chewed on the ropes. At last, the lion was free!

"I will surely win," laughed Hare,

"for I am fast and you are slow."

"We will see," said Tortoise.

2

The Tortoise and the Hare

A Retelling of the Aesop's Fable

A

Soon Hare was far ahead.

"I can't lose," he said, so he lay down to

take a nap. Snooze, snooze, snooze.

5

B

All the animals cheered.

"How did you ever beat Hare?" asked Horse.

"He may be fast," said Tortoise. "But slow

and steady wins the race!"

❀ The End ❀

7

On the day of the big race, all the animals came to watch.

"On your mark, get set, go!" said Frog.

GO!

Once upon a time, Tortoise and Hare decided to have a race.

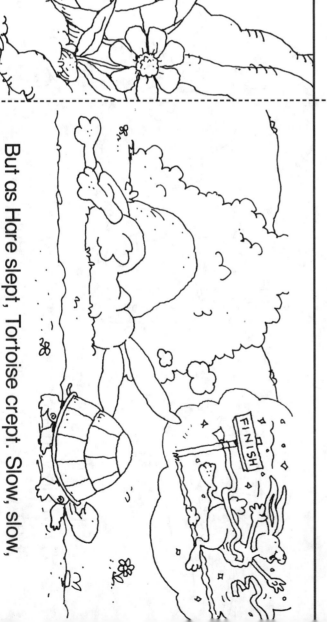

Hare hopped. Fast, fast, fast. Tortoise crept. Slow, slow, slow.

But as Hare slept, Tortoise crept. Slow, slow, slow. After a while, he passed Hare. Then he crossed the finish line!

FINISH

Hans Christian Andersen

Mini-Books

One stormy night, there was a knock on the door. "Hello," said a messy girl with wet hair and muddy clothes. "I am a real princess. Can I stay here tonight?"

2

B

The Princess and the Pea
A Retelling of the Hans Christian Andersen Tale

A

The next morning, he asked the princess how she had slept. "Badly!" she said with a yawn. "It felt like there was a bowling ball under the mattresses!"

5

The girl said yes, of course. Then they both lived, and snoozed, happily ever after.

❀ *The End* ❀

7

The prince invited her in and gave her a cup of hot cocoa. Could she be a real princess? He had a plan to find out.

3

The prince piled 20 mattresses on top of 20 quilts. Then, under it all, he put a tiny pea. "Here is your bed. Sweet dreams!" he said.

4

Once upon a time, a prince decided it was time to wed. He looked high and low for the perfect wife, but had no luck. He could not find a real princess anywhere.

1

With that, the prince asked the girl to marry him at once. For only a real princess could feel a tiny pea under 20 mattresses and 20 quilts.

6

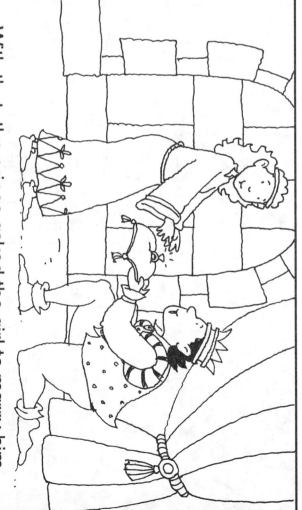

2

Out popped five tiny ducklings. Four were fluffy and cute. One was gray and ugly.

B

The Ugly Duckling
A Retelling of the Hans Christian Andersen Tale

A

At last, Ugly Duckling came to a lake filled with beautiful swans. When they swam near, he hid his face under his wing.

5

Why, Ugly Duckling had grown into a beautiful swan, just like them! After that, he lived happily ever after and was always kind to all living things—from peacocks to potato bugs.

❈ *The End* ❈

7

The cute ducklings teased their ugly brother.
They pecked at him. They ate his bread.
They said, "We don't like you. Go away!"

One day, Ugly Duckling did leave. But
the new birds he met were nasty, too.
They said, "We don't like you. Go away!"

Once upon a time, a mother duck's eggs began to
hatch. Crack! Crack! Crack! Crack! Crack!

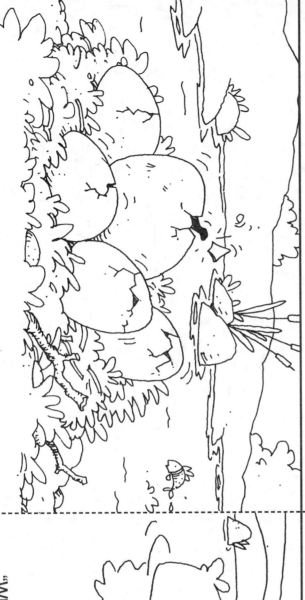

"Why are you so shy?" asked one. "Have you
looked in a mirror lately?" At that, Ugly
Duckling peered into the silver water.

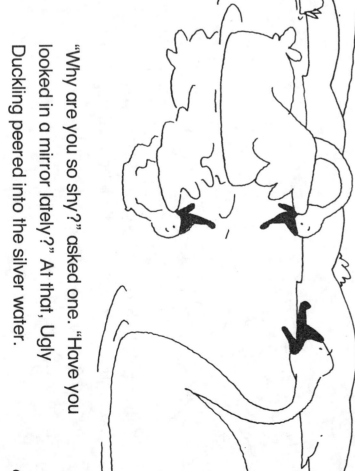

"Come here!" he shouted to the boy. With

13   shaking knees, the child did as he was told.

One day, a swindler came to town. He told

the king he would make him the finest suit

2   ever seen. And it would be magic, too!

B

The Emperor's New Clothes

A Retelling of the Hans Christian Andersen Tale

A

After that, the king put on a fluffy bathrobe.

Then he marched proudly on . . . with that

smart little boy right by his side.

❦ *The End* ❦

15

Only wise people would be able to see the suit. The unwise would think it was invisible.

3

All the people gasped. The king gasped, too.

12

Once upon a time, there lived a king who loved fancy clothes.

1

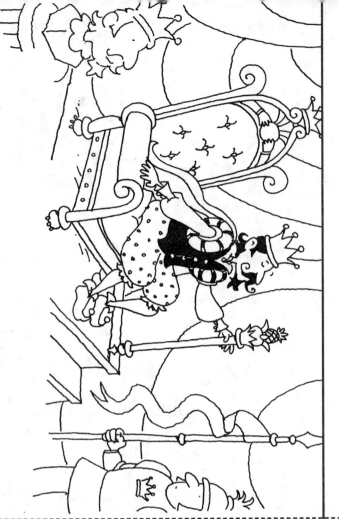

"Thanks for telling me the truth. That makes you the wisest person of all!" said the king.

14

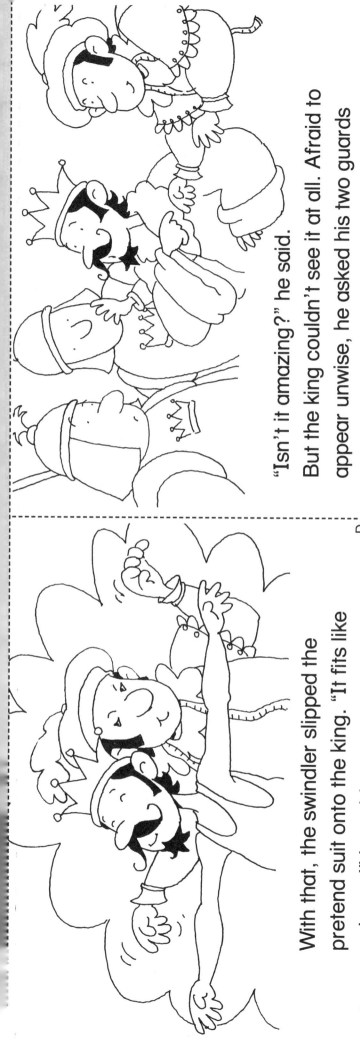

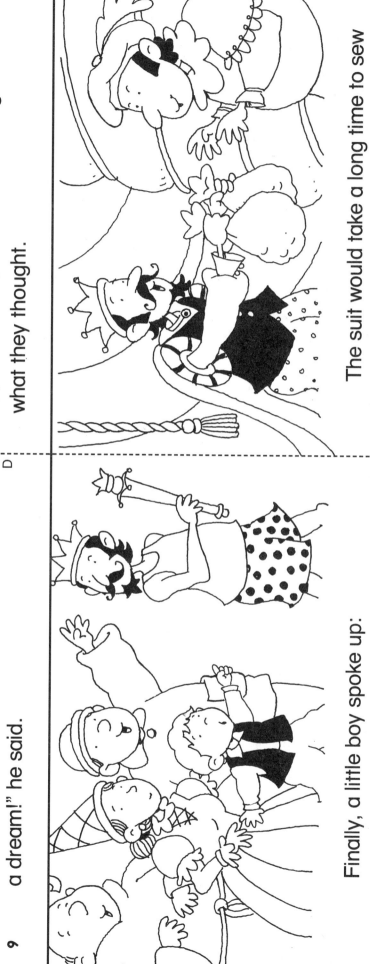

"Isn't it amazing?" he said.
But the king couldn't see it at all. Afraid to
appear unwise, he asked his two guards
what they thought.

9

The suit would take a long time to sew
and cost two big bags of gold! But, the
king had to have it, so he agreed.

4

With that, the swindler slipped the
pretend suit onto the king. "It fits like
a dream!" he said.

9

Finally, a little boy spoke up:
"I don't get it. The king isn't wearing
anything but his underwear!"

11

D

C

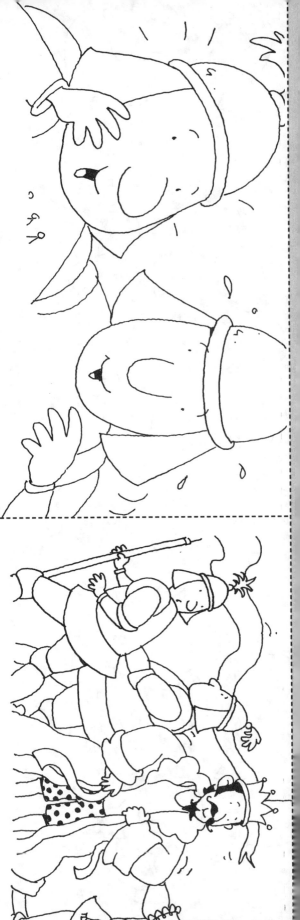

7

But the guards couldn't see it either!

"I like the fabric," lied one.

"I like the buttons," lied the other.

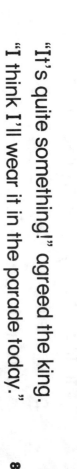

8

"It's quite something!" agreed the king.

"I think I'll wear it in the parade today."

5

After many weeks, the outfit was finished.
The swindler brought it to the palace and
pretended to hold it up in the air.

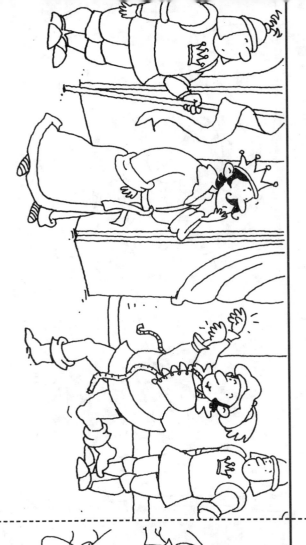

10

During the parade, the king marched
proudly through town. Afraid to appear
unwise, everyone yelled,
"Unbelievable!" and "One of a kind!"

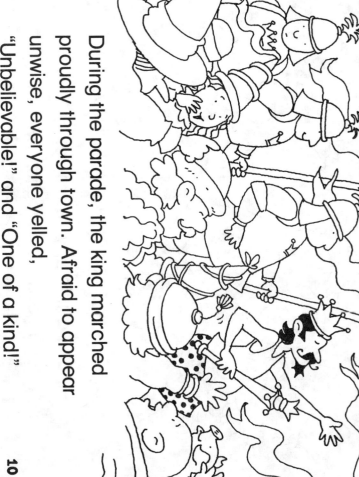

The Brothers Grimm

Mini-Books

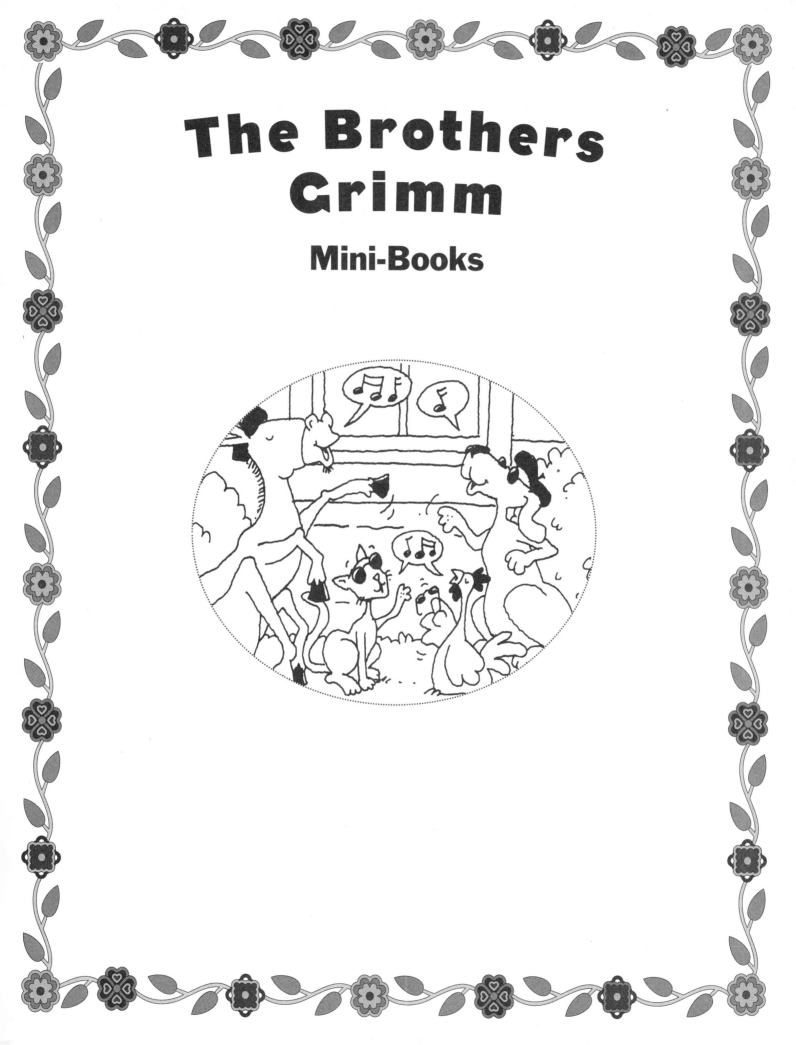

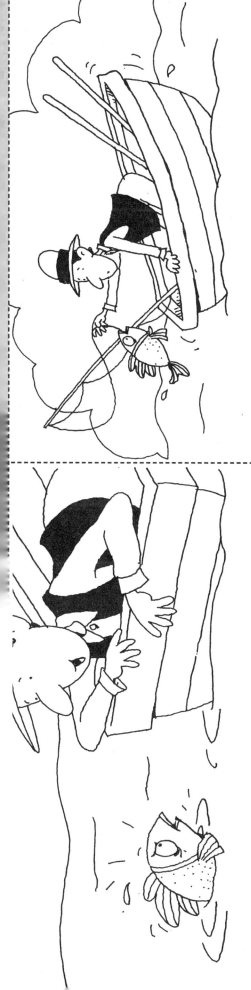

One day, the man caught a magical fish
who begged, "Let me go, I'll grant your wish!"
So the man unhooked the fish from his line,
saying, "There is nothing I need, my life is fine."

2

B

The Fisherman and His Wife

A Retelling of the Brothers Grimm Tale

A

So the next day, the man called out to the fish:
"Commanding the sky, that is our wish!"
"Enough!" cried the fish, "I'm sick of your greed.
I've done some thinking, I know what you need."

13

This is the tale of the fisherman and his wife.
In their hut by the sea, they had a great life.

❀ The End ❀

15

3

That night, when he told his wife of the fish,
she said, "Life is superb, but I DO have a wish.
We could really use a brand-new house
with plenty of cupboards and nary a mouse."

1

This is the tale of the fisherman and his wife.
In their hut by the sea, they had a great life.

The wife said, "We must rule the moon and sun.
Ordering them around would sure be fun."

12

Zip, zap, zowie! Everything vanished!
The castle, the subjects, and all they had wished!
But to tell the truth, the couple wasn't mad,
for they'd missed the simple life they'd had.

14

The wife said, "We now need a castle of stone
with a silver staircase and a golden phone."

6

D

So the next day, the man called out to the fish:
"A tidy new house, that is our wish!"

4

C

The wife said, "We now need some people to rule.
Without any subjects, I feel quite the fool."

9

Zip, zap, zowie! Their dream came true.
But by and by, it just wouldn't do.

11

So the next day, the man called out to the fish:
"A fabulous castle, that is our wish!"

Zip, zap, zowie! Their dream came true.
But by and by, it just wouldn't do.

Zip, zap, zowie! Their dream came true.
But by and by, it just wouldn't do.

So the next day, the man called out to the fish:
"People to boss, that is our wish!"

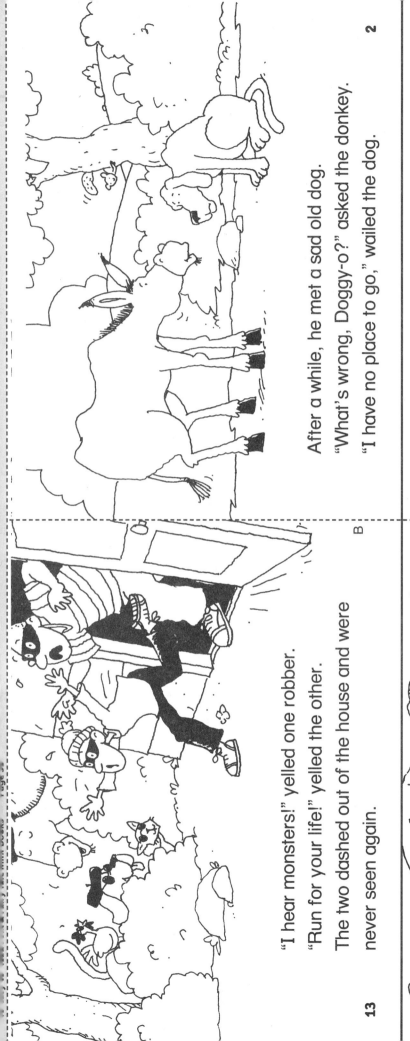

The Bremen Town Musicians
A Retelling of the Brothers Grimm Tale

A

After a while, he met a sad old dog.

"What's wrong, Doggy-o?" asked the donkey.

"I have no place to go," wailed the dog.

B

2

"I hear monsters!" yelled one robber.

"Run for your life!" yelled the other.

The two dashed out of the house and were

never seen again.

13

After that, the animals made the house their home. And the band played happily ever after.

❀ The End ❀

15

3

"Come join my band," said the donkey.

"Cool!" said the dog.

Then the two set out for town.

1

Long ago, there lived a donkey with a big problem. When he became too old to work, his owner kicked him off the farm. Not knowing what else to do, he set out for Bremen Town. He still had a nice vioce. Maybe he could form a band.

12

"I have a plan. Strike up the band!" said the donkey.

"COCK-A-DOODLE-DO! MEOW! BOW-WOW! BRAY!" they sang loudly.

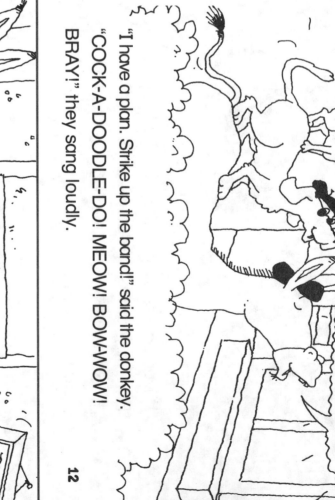

14

In went the four friends. First, they ate a fine meal. Next, they returned the money to the bank and became town heroes.

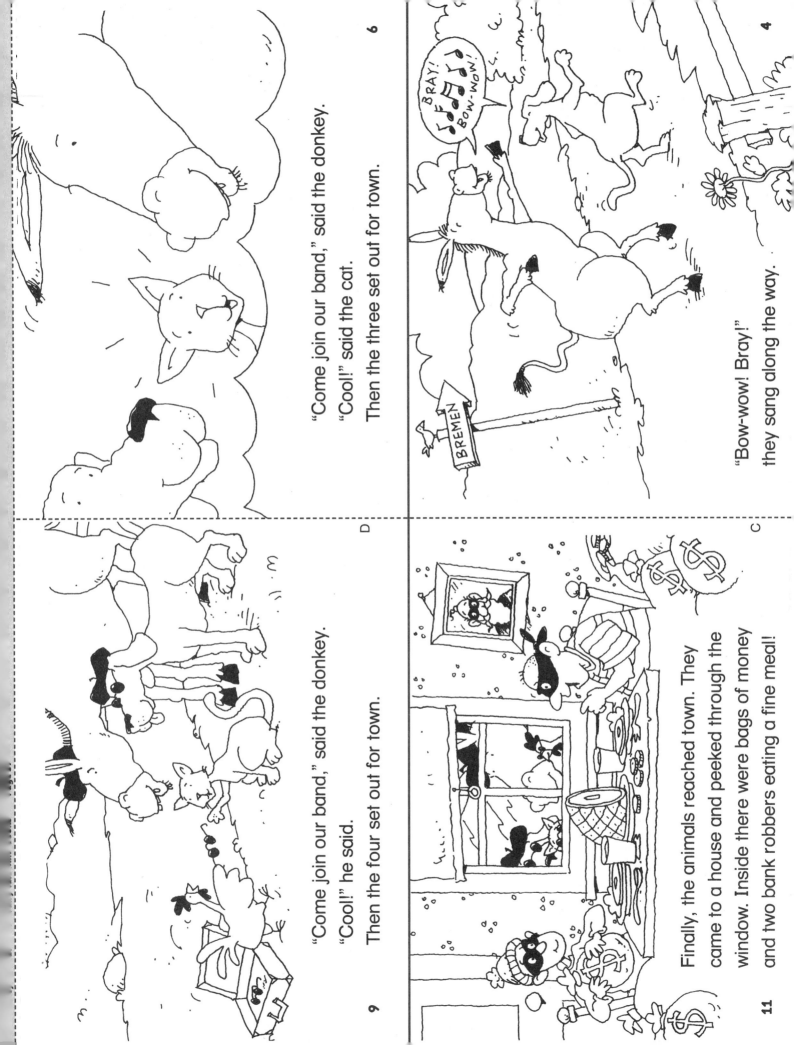

"Come join our band," said the donkey.
"Cool!" said the cat.
Then the three set out for town.

6

D

"Bow-wow! Bray!"
they sang along the way.

4

C

"Come join our band," said the donkey.
"Cool!" he said.
Then the four set out for town.

9

Finally, the animals reached town. They came to a house and peeked through the window. Inside there were bags of money and two bank robbers eating a fine meal!

11

"Meow! Bow-wow! Bray!"
they sang along the way.

After a while, they met a sad old cat.
"What's wrong, Kitty-o?" asked the donkey.
"I have no place to go," wailed the cat.

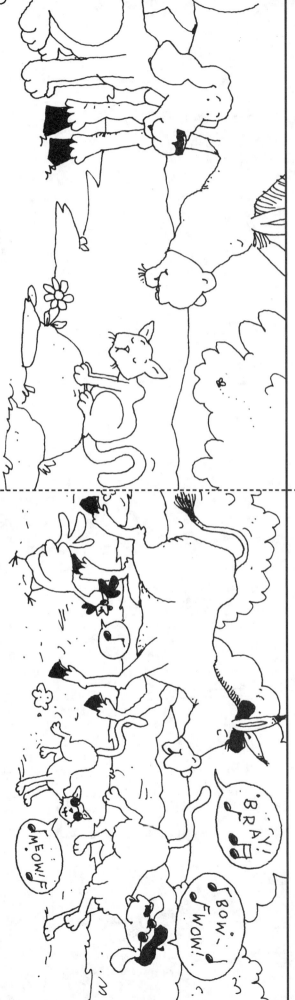

After a while, they met a sad old rooster.
"What's wrong, Rooster-o?" asked the donkey.
"I have no place to go," wailed the rooster.

"Cock-a-Doodle-do! Meow! Bow-wow!
Bray!" they sang along the way.

Mother Goose

Mini-Books

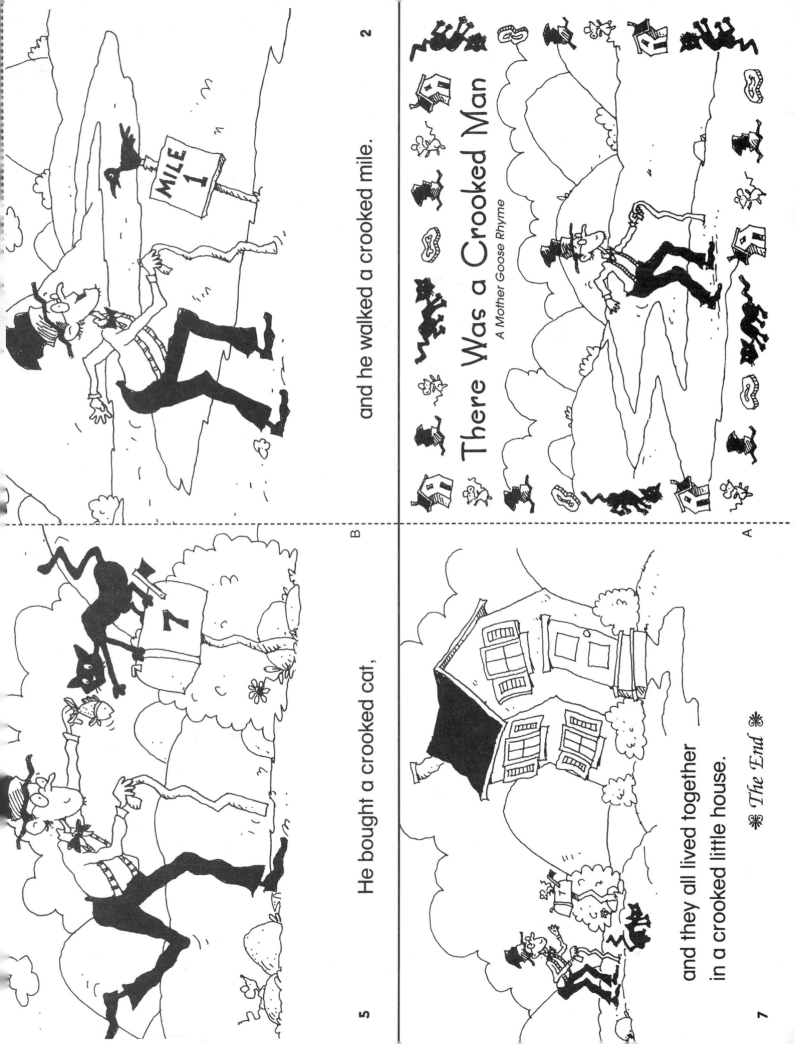

2

and he walked a crooked mile.

B

There Was a Crooked Man
A Mother Goose Rhyme

A

5

He bought a crooked cat,

7

and they all lived together
in a crooked little house.

❀ The End ❀

3 He found a crooked sixpence

1 There was a crooked man,

4 against a crooked stile.

6 which caught a crooked mouse.

There Was an Old Woman

There was an old woman
Who lived in a shoe.
She had so many children,
She didn't know what to do.

B

2

Poems for Your Pocket
Favorite Mother Goose Rhymes

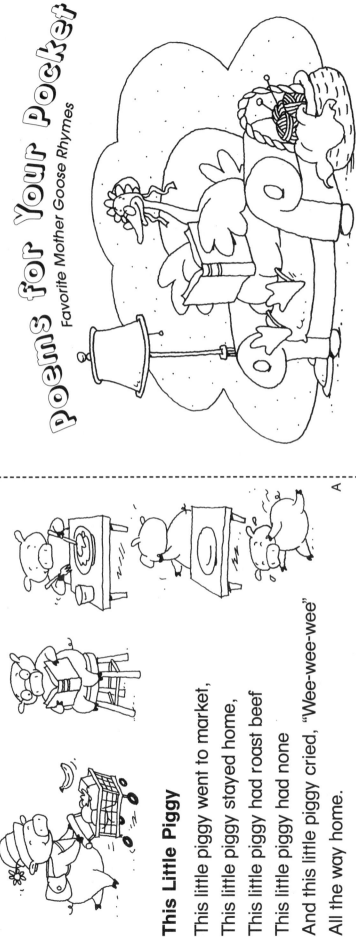

A

Little Miss Muffet

Little Miss Muffet
Sat on her tuffet,
Eating her curds and whey.

5

This Little Piggy

This little piggy went to market,
This little piggy stayed home,
This little piggy had roast beef
This little piggy had none
And this little piggy cried, "Wee-wee-wee"
All the way home.

7

Hey, Diddle, Diddle

Hey, diddle, diddle,
The cat and the fiddle,
The cow jumped over the moon.

3

Humpty Dumpty

Humpty Dumpty sat on the wall.
Humpty Dumpty had a great fall.
All the king's horses and all the king's men,
Couldn't put Humpty together again.

1

The little dog laughed
To see such a sport,
And the dish ran away
With the spoon.

4

Along came a spider
And sat down beside her
And frightened Miss Muffet away.

6